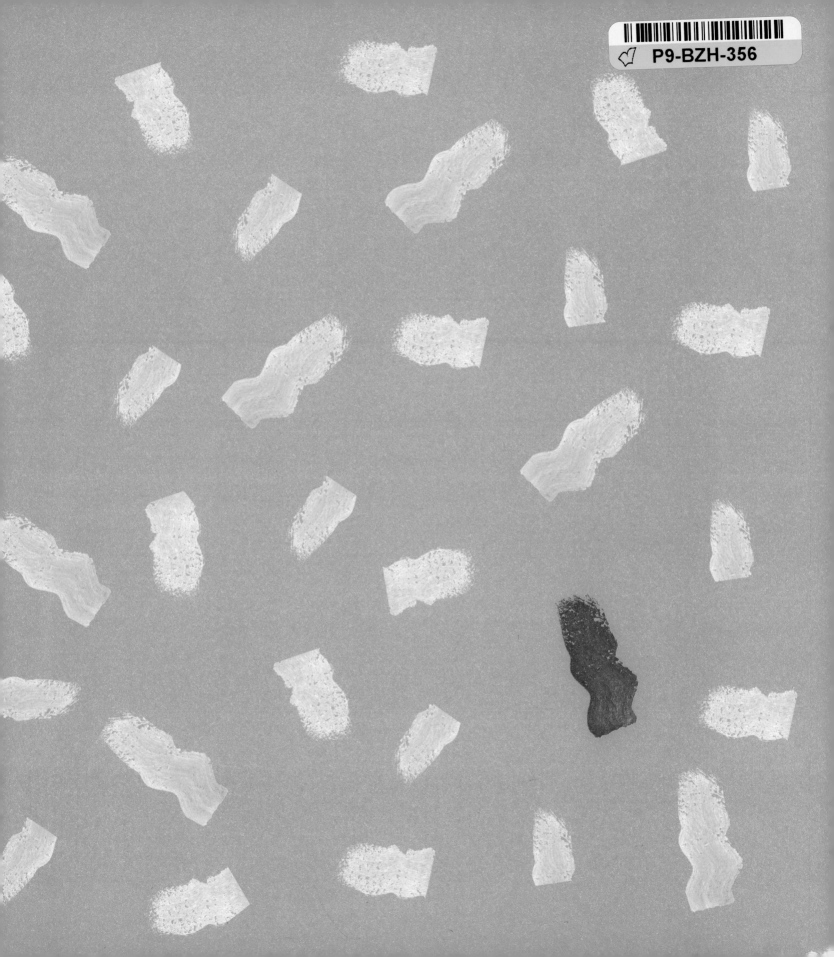

P9-BZH-356

Hello.

My name is George and I am an artist.

I have been painting since I was five.
I paint pictures of things I like.

One of my favorite things to paint is Blue Dog.

Why is Blue Dog blue?

Artists don't have to paint things the way they really are.

I use my imagination to paint my own world.
I can paint a dog any color I can imagine.

So why is Blue Dog blue?

Well, the truth is that Blue Dog isn't always blue.

Sometimes, I paint Blue Dog

red.

Other times, I paint Blue Dog

Occasionally, I paint BLUE DOG

Once in a while, I paint Blue Dog

I never paint Blue Dog

yellow.

green ().

orange.

purple (except for when I do).

I can paint
a Blue Dog
rainbow.

But most of the time,
I paint Blue Dog blue.

Which

brings

us

back

to the

same

question.

WHY
IS BLUE DOG
BLUE?

Maybe it has to do with
WHAT I THINK ABOUT
when I paint.

What color do I paint
Blue Dog

when I go FISHING?

salmon

What color do I paint Blue Dog when I

want a hot dog?

mustard

What color do I paint Blue Dog when I

bake a pie?

cherry

What color do I paint Blue Dog when I

go to the bEach?

tan

What color

do I paint

Blue Dog

when I

fall

in

the

swamp?

moss green

magenta

lavender

What other colors can I paint Blue Dog?

auburn

chartreuse

ebony

khaki

turquoise

emerald

mauve

cajun

burgundy

apricot

violet

periwinkle

alabaster

avocado

aqua

chocolate

gray

Very pretty, but still not blue. **Blue Dog is blue.**

sky!

Why? Why? Why? Look in the

Blue Dog is every

where, like the sky.

That's why.

BY GEORGE RODRIGUE
TEXT WITH BRUCE GOLDSTONE

George Rodrigue was born in
New Iberia, Louisiana. For more than
twenty-five years he has painted
scenes of Cajun life. He started
painting Blue Dog in the 1980s,
partly inspired by a frisky
terrier/spaniel and the legendary
loup garou. His mother told him
the story of this mythic Cajun
werewolf dog when he was a child.
George's Blue Dog has captured
the hearts and imaginations of
people around the world. Today,
he paints in Lafayette, Louisiana
and Carmel, California. Visit
Blue Dog Kids at the artist's website
(www.bluedogart.com) to find out
more about him and see how
Blue Dog has inspired some kids
to create their own art.

Bruce Goldstone lives in New York City with
a multi-colored menagerie of pets. He is often
covered in lime-green and yellow parakeet
feathers, black-and-brown dog fur, and
white-and-orange cat hair. He's also the author
of two children's books, *The Beastly Feast*
and *Ten Friends* and co-author with celebrated
mime Marcel Marceau of *Bip in a Book*.

Published by
Stewart, Tabori & Chang
An imprint of Harry N. Abrams, Inc.

Text and art copyright © 2001 George Rodrigue
Text with Bruce Goldstone

All rights reserved. No portion of this book may be
reproduced, stored in a retrieval system, or transmitted
in any form or by any means, mechanical, electronic,
photocopying, recording, or otherwise, without written
permission from the publisher.

Library of Congress Cataloging-in-Publication Data
Rodrigue, George
Why is blue dog blue? / by George Rodrigue ;
text with Bruce Goldstone.
p. cm.
ISBN-13: 978-1-58479-162-1
ISBN-10: 1-58479-162-4
1.Color in art. 2. Tiffany (Dog) I. Goldstone, Bruce.
II. Title.

ND1490 .R63 2002
701'.85—dc21

2001057624

The text of this book was composed in
Bodoni Book and Frutiger.

Printed and bound in China
10 9 8 7 6 5

Design by Alexander Isley Inc.
Project Editor: Sandy Gilbert
Production: Kim Tyner

HNA ■■■□□□
harry n. abrams, inc.
a subsidiary of La Martinière Groupe
115 West 18th Street
New York, NY 10011
www.hnabooks.com

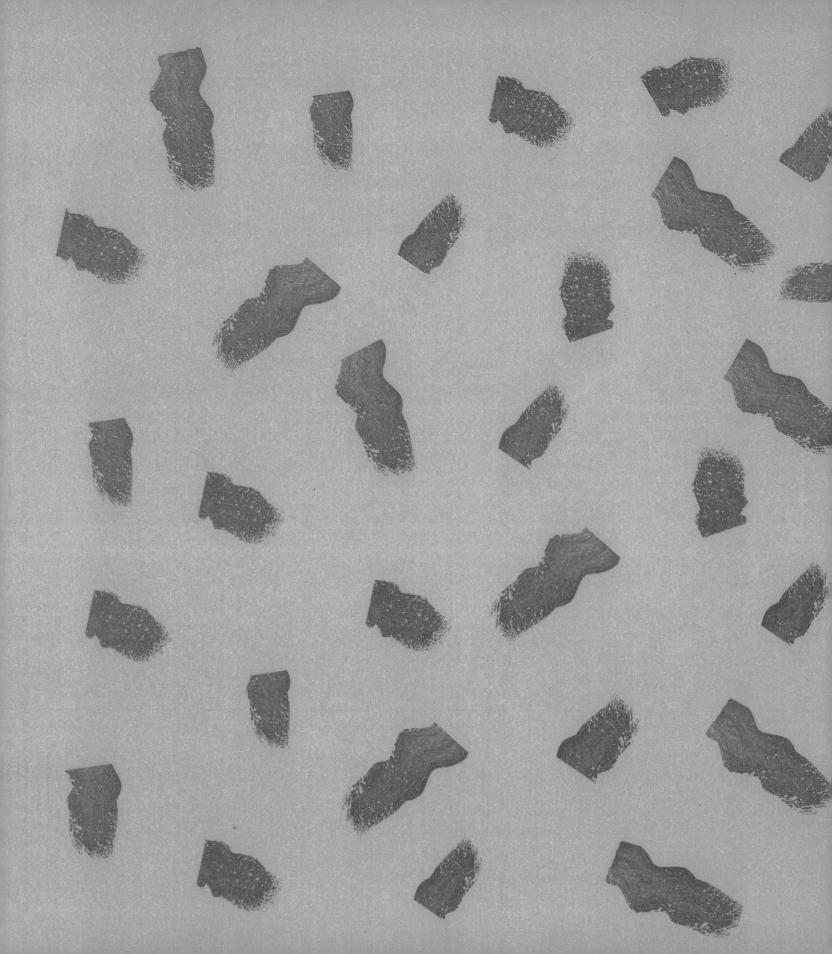